THE WISHING FIELD

Aspen Faraway

HSP
Published by Haven Street Publishing
www.havenstreetpublishing.com

Contents

Chapter One

Even right up until the middle of her party, Ivory Samson still expected the doorbell to ring, and a deliveryman would be standing there with a beautifully wrapped package for her. Gramma Del always sent her something special on her birthdays.

"Gramma Del will probably get me something really special this year," Ivory had said just yesterday to her mother. "Thirteen is a very special birthday."

"Don't count on it," Jill Samson had told her daughter gently. "Gramma Del hasn't been feeling well lately. I doubt she's been able to get you something."

"But, Mom," Ivory had protested. "Gramma Del always gets the best presents."

The conversation had ended then as her mother seemed to drift away into her own special birthday memories of Gramma Del.

For the three days leading up to her birthday, Ivory hadn't left the house. She wasn't taking any chances on missing Gramma Del's special gift. She made sure her mother checked the mail at least twice a day.

Although Gramma Del lived just on the edge of the small town of Digby, Nova Scotia, she still had her special presents delivered. Although Ivory knew the presents only came from about a mile away, the deliveryman carried the excitement for her as if they'd been picked up in Japan. Last year it had been a cute baby bunny with brown floppy ears, nestled snuggly in a wicker basket, complete with his own birth certificate. Ivory had squealed in an instant maternal excitement.

"Honey, we have to start your party now," her mother pleaded at seven o'clock when the living room had been filled with seven twelve- and thirteen-year-old girls.

"But let's just wait for five more minutes," Ivory pleaded.

"Why?" her mother asked. "If it's because you're still expecting something from Gramma Del, she already sent you a card. I picked it up at the mail this afternoon. I was going to give it to you at your party."

"A card!" Ivory exclaimed in dismay. Gramma Del never gave her a card in her life! It was always a really exciting present. "Are you sure it was from Gramma Del?"

"Well, I've known my mother for thirty-seven years and I'd know her handwriting by now," her mother answered with just a hint of sarcasm.

"But what about the present?" Ivory whined, aware that she sounded like she was three instead of thirteen.

"I told you, she hasn't been well lately, Ivory," her mom's voice became impatient. "Don't be so selfish. The woman is seventy-nine years old!"

Ivory felt her face grow hot. She hadn't meant to not care about Gramma Del. But it was just that she'd always expected that when she became a teenager, Gramma Del's presents would just become, well, more special.

With her brother, Rayne, away for the night at his friend's house, Ivory and her friends had the whole house to themselves, except for her mom's office off the kitchen. Her mother had said this would be a good time to work on her book, but Ivory just bet that the real reason she remained downstairs was to keep an eye on the group.

By eight-thirty, when the other girls could not wait for one more minute to watch the movies and eat their pizza, Ivory gave in and began opening presents. Her mom came out of the office with a large box. Maybe her mother had been holding out with Gramma Del's present after all.

Ivory blushed as her friends sang Happy Birthday to her. She hated being the center of attention. She was always unsure of what to do, who to look at, even what expression was appropriate on her face for the duration of the song. It always seemed longer when she was the recipient of the serenade than when she was singing it to some other victim. That was the worst part of birthdays, she decided while they sang. Next year, she promised herself, she would outlaw that song at her parties and get right to the presents.

Her best friend, Cassie Edwards gave her a DVD of their favorite band, Dayton. Ivory secretly expected she'd killed two birds with one stone, having wanted to get the video for herself, but needing to spend her allowance on a present for Ivory.

"Ooh, let's watch that instead of the other movie," was the general voice of the party.

Christine and Courtney Marshall, the twins from across the street, who weren't really her friends anyway, gave Ivory a set of earrings.

Jenna Murphy, a girl in her class, gave her a bathing suit. "If it doesn't fit, my mom says she'll exchange it for you."

"Thanks," Ivory feigned appreciation and set the garment on top of the earrings and the DVD.

Rachel and Dana, other girls from her class at school, gave her lipstick and nail polish. The lipstick was a dark red and she couldn't imagine where she would wear it, except maybe for next Halloween when she needed fake blood. But, she felt kinda good, being old enough to receive lipstick for a present. The nail polish was an emerald green, just like Cassie's. This was great!

Lucy Davies gave Ivory a package of different colored hair scrunchies. Ivory was glad, because she was tired of wearing her long brown ponytail pulled back with the same black band she'd worn all year long as her hair had grown out from a bob to down below her shoulders.

The big box from her mother's office turned out to be a laptop! It was a present from her mom and dad. Now she wouldn't have to use her mother's computer in limited spurts.

"Dad sends you hugs and kisses," her mother said apologetically. Her dad was an actor and had been in the city of Halifax for the past three weeks working on a movie. She knew he wouldn't be home at least all summer, and she missed him. She wished he'd at least called to say happy birthday.

With the presents opened, and everyone's fingernails and toenails painted green, the girls settled onto sleeping bags to watch movies and eat pizza and junk food. Ivory couldn't help feeling haunted by the void created by her dad and Gramma Del.

She remembered when she'd turned five, Gramma Del had given her the most special gift she'd ever received. She had taken her down to a large field behind her house, and Ivory remembered how she had squealed with delight when she saw the millions of sparkles in the field.

"It's a wishing field," Gramma Del had explained with a sparkle reflected in her emerald eyes. "Make any wish you like for your birthday."

"I want a baby brother!" Five year old Ivory had declared without a moment's hesitation.

"Oh no," Gramma Del had laughed in surprise. "I don't think wishing for something alive counts. It has to be for something like a doll or a toy. Come on, make another wish."

"But I want a baby brother," Ivory had insisted, dismayed at the field's limitations.

She smiled now when she remembered her grandmother's patience with her. Hand in hand, they'd walked out of that field with Ivory holding a firm belief in her wish.

The next day a doll, a baby boy doll, dressed in real baby clothes and wrapped in a real baby blanket lay in a little wicker bassinet beside her bed when she woke up. A birth certificate, created by her grandmother, told her that he was her baby "brother" and she could name him whatever she wanted. She named him Jimmy and dragged him everywhere with her.

A few months later, her mom and dad had sat her down and told her very seriously that she was going to be a big sister. They were going to have a baby, they said. Several months later, a lot of months to little Ivory, her real baby brother was born and her parents named him Rayne. Ivory had changed Jimmy's name to Rayne too, and when her mom was still in the hospital with her real baby brother, she'd enjoyed the summer days with her grandmother.

After several failed attempts to escape her grandmother's watchful eye, the little girl had finally managed to sneak back to the wishing field. But all the sparkles had vanished.

Chapter Two

Ivory sat at her desk in her bedroom, twirling the pen aimlessly. The rain pelting her window refused her the concentration she needed to begin her new story. She'd thought this one up in the early hours of the morning when the lightning and thunder had awakened her. Now she couldn't find the right opening words.

Finally she slammed the pen down on her desk in frustration and went across the tiny pink room and flopped on her bed. It had rained for three days, ever since the night of her birthday party, and she just couldn't take one more day inside.

She closed her eyes and tried to remember the last time she'd set foot outside of her house. That would've been on the day of the party. And even then, she'd only gone to the end of her driveway to glance up and down the street to make sure no courier guy would arrive at the door while she took a brief trip to the bathroom. Even on that day, the air had been cool and damp. Usual for at least one third of the summer days in Nova Scotia, she estimated.

Ivory rolled over and stared at her white ceiling and pictured the hot sun of a balmy day in Hawaii or Florida. She wished she were rich. If she ever did get rich one day, she promised herself she would leave Nova Scotia and move to a place where it was hot and sunny every single day of the year. Like California, maybe. Since her dad was an actor, maybe she could talk him into moving them to Hollywood. Maybe she'd become a famous movie star. She held up her still green fingernails in front of her and imagined how gold and diamond rings would look on every single finger.

She heard the phone ring and heard her mother walk across the kitchen floor to answer it. Maybe it was Dad. She'd ask him right here and now if they could move to Hollywood. It would probably take a while to convince him, so the sooner she started, the better.

She leaped off her bed and ran out the door. She ran down the stairs. "If it's Dad, I want to talk to him!" she shouted over the banister.

Her mother came out of the kitchen and looked up at her with a worried expression. Ivory knew something was wrong.

"It's Gramma Del," her mother said seriously. "She's sick and may have to go to the hospital. Keep an eye on Rayne, and I'll call if I have to take her in."

Ivory stood frozen on the second step. She couldn't remember Gramma Del ever being sick in her life! What if Gramma Del was going to die? She was old; very old. What if she just died from being too old? She knew Cassie's grandparents were both dead, but she never expected anything could ever happen to her own grandmother.

She went back up to her room, but her earlier visions of grandeur eluded her. She couldn't feel good about anything while wondering how sick her grandmother was. Her mom hadn't even told her what kind of sick. Migraine sick? Gramma Del used to have migraines a few years ago. Was she sick with a cold or flu? Probably not in the summer, but then again, with old people, you never knew.

She imagined her mother taking Gramma Del into outpatients and going through the usual routine of explaining that Gramma Del's name *is* Philadelphia and that she is *not from* Philadelphia. She'd been through that ritual a million times herself; having to spell Ivory for perfectly literate people. Same with Rayne. She hoped her family wouldn't expect her first child to be named something weird like Sunbeam or something. She had decided long ago that if she had a son when she grew up, she would name him Tommy, and if she ever had a daughter, she would name her Ashley. Her decision had been based on her undying love for a boy in her class since third grade, Tommy Ashley. Tommy Ashley took Ivory's mind off of Gramma Del, but only for a moment.

She remembered the silly, childish thing she'd done just last summer. She'd gone to visit Gramma Del for the day and she'd gone in search of the wishing field again. She was going to wish that she and Tommy would get married someday. While she was at it, she was going to wish Maple Evans moved away, because as long as she was around, no boy would even notice Ivory Samson or any other girl in the whole Digby Elementary School. But now in September, she'd be starting Junior High, and she knew she'd have more competition than just Maple Evans.

She remembered how the summer before, she'd just found a barren, rocky field in place of her earlier magical experience. She'd searched painstakingly for a tiny sparkle, anything that would prove she hadn't just dreamed up the whole thing in her wild imagination, like her parents insisted she had. She knew she'd seen sparkles there when she was five, she just knew it! Gramma Del just looked at her with a twinkle in her eye instead of telling her parents the truth. All Ivory was left with was a memory. Perhaps even only a memory of a dream. An hour of searching in that field last summer hadn't even turned up the faintest hint of fool's gold or even broken glass. There was absolutely nothing in that field that promised glitter. She'd even made sure she'd gone back at noon, precisely the time of her original visit to the field years ago.

The phone rang, bringing her back up out of the past. She reached for her cell phone on her nightstand.

"I'm at the hospital," her mom spoke in a monotone of information. "I'm going to be here for a while. There's leftovers in the fridge you can heat up in the microwave for you and Rayne for supper."

"How's Gramma Del?"

Ivory heard a choke in her mother's voice. "She's not very good, honey. She had pneumonia and suffered a stroke when I brought her in."

Ivory felt her skin turn to ice. She couldn't believe this was happening. Gramma Del was so healthy. She was always walking, and she always bragged about being fit as a fiddle.

Ivory hung up with a sinking feeling. She couldn't bear to consider all the possibilities. Gramma Del couldn't die! She was too vibrant and alive to die. She would probably be up and around in a week or two, knowing Gramma Del. Maybe she could come live with them when she got out of the hospital. That would be great having Gramma Del around all the time.

She forced the subject out of her mind as she went down to rummage through the fridge to prepare dinner for Rayne and herself.

Chapter Three

After a dull supper of reheated spaghetti, Ivory and Rayne sat in the living room in front of rerunning sitcoms and waited for Uncle Paul. He'd agreed to spend the night with them while their mother remained at the hospital.

"I don't know why he has to come anyway," Ivory protested over the phone. "I'm thirteen. I'm old enough to baby-sit."

"Not at night," her mother argued, her tone warning Ivory to let the issue go. Ivory let it go grudgingly. She knew Cassie babysat for the Hamiltons until two or three o'clock in the morning some weekends. What would be the difference? But she also knew her mother had a lot on her mind, and it would be best to let it rest. The issue of being over-protected could be discussed when Gramma Del was safely at home, probably tomorrow or the next day.

Uncle Paul was Ivory's dad's brother. Very boring to say the least. Ivory admitted all the exciting relatives came from her mother's side of the family. Uncle Paul was a mapmaker and got to fly in helicopters and airplanes. That was the only interesting thing about Uncle Paul. He wasn't even married because he was so boring. Even his looks were boring. He wasn't ugly; in fact, he was quite good looking, but the kind of good looking that was expected. Sort of perfect. Not one interesting characteristic about his face. Or his hair. Everything was predictable; every hair always in place. He wasn't fat; he wasn't thin. He looked exactly as one would expect a person to look if they were to imagine one. Straight teeth, straight hair, good posture, no bad habits. Just plain boring.

He even arrived in a boring way. He called to say he'd be there in five minutes. When he arrived five minutes later, he was boring. He told Rayne that eight o'clock was a good bedtime for an eight year old, and he should go to bed. He brought some maps to work on at the kitchen table and basically ignored Ivory.

"I'll sleep on the couch, " he said pleasantly. "Why don't you go call your friends, or do whatever it is that teenage girls do?"

She went up to her room, annoyed at being dismissed so easily in her own home, but feeling a sort of maturity at being recognized as a teenager and expected to look after herself. At least he hadn't come in and expected to take over and treat her like a baby.

She went to her room and called Cassie, but Cassie was out with her older sister, Sasha. Ever since Cassie had turned thirteen and started her period a few months ago, her sister had sort of taken her under her wing after ignoring her for the first thirteen years of her life. While Cassie was basking in the sudden attention, Ivory had been left by the wayside, still waiting for the forces of nature to wreak havoc on her own body.

She lay on her bed and stared at her ceiling, now taking on a yellowish tinge from the glow of her bedside lamp. She wondered if her period would ever start. As soon as she'd turned eleven, she'd feared the event for a whole year, just because Maple Evans had gotten hers the day before school started in fifth grade.

As more and more girls got theirs, Ivory's dread of the

event turned to desire. As sixth grade wore on and her friends proudly announced their developing bodies, as if they were personally responsible for the process, Ivory began to worry if she were normal. Even though Miss Phinney, the Health teacher, warned the class that every girl was different and some didn't start until they were fifteen or sixteen, Ivory knew she wasn't "normal".

Ivory's only consolation during sixth grade was the fact that she was not alone. Cassie and two other girls hadn't started. But during March Break, Cassie had called her excitedly to announce her great news, and Ivory was certain that both of the other girls would probably get theirs this summer. On the last day of school they had both been wearing bras.

Ivory had two flowery, lacy bras that Gramma Del had given her last Christmas, but she still had no reason to wear them. When she had tried, it had only resulted in two triangles of wrinkles bumping up under her shirt. She knew everybody else could notice them and her whole bra-wearing experience had ended in less than five minutes. She'd decided to save them for future use, when and if she ever needed them, and crammed the tiny things into the back of her underwear drawer; refusing to be constantly reminded that they were of no use to her.

Ivory closed her eyes and wondered what it would be like to have a period. All the girls that talked about it in hushed whispers during recess claimed it made them feel like a woman. What did feeling like a woman feel like? She hadn't noticed any changes in the behavior of any of those giggling girls. The obnoxious ones were just as obnoxious and the nice ones were just as nice. She had been sure she'd be initiated into that group of "women" by now. On Tuesday when she'd turned thirteen, she'd stayed awake all night, expecting her period to magically start, but it hadn't. Why did she have to be the only girl in her entire grade who still looked like a boy from the neck down? It just wasn't fair.

She got up and opened her closet door and looked at the twenty-five brown paper bags stacked neatly on the top shelf. Nearly every Friday for six months or so, Gramma Del had dropped off the brown bag for Ivory. The first bag had been opened immediately with curiosity in front of her father and slammed shut in embarrassment when she saw its contents. Feminine Napkins, the square box read.

"You'll be needing them any day," Gramma Del had warned.

Ivory had looked forward to those bags as sort of a confirmation that one day something really would happen. But nothing did. And the brown paper bags just kept piling up in the top of her closet. This was the first Friday in months that Gramma Del hadn't brought by the bag.

Thinking of Gramma Del reminded Ivory of the card she'd been too selfish to open on her birthday. Ivory felt a tear spring to her big brown eyes as she regretted her selfishness. She closed the closet door and went to the pile of envelopes and papers on her desk. Tears rolled down her cheeks as she opened the envelope.

Chapter Four

Ivory pulled out the large paper card. It was brownish yellow with a hand-drawn map of Digby on it. Ivory opened it up and saw that the map continued onto the back of the card. She looked inside the card, and a brief handwritten verse captured her interest.

HAPPY THIRTEENTH BIRTHDAY, IVORY
THIS IS YOUR BIGGEST BIRTHDAY YET!
THE TREASURE OF THIS MAP MUST BE
THE BIGGEST PRESENT YOU COULD GET!

Puzzled, Ivory unfolded the paper card and spread the map out on her bed. Yes, it was clearly a map of the town. But none of the places were labeled; just squares and streets. Even the streets weren't labeled, but with only about twenty streets in the town, it was clear to tell which were which.

"A treasure map," Ivory whispered, and her tears stopped. She turned it over and read the verse again. Gramma Del had gotten her a present after all! Ivory knew Gramma Del would never forget such an important birthday. Had she left the special gift here where the big red X was? Well, that was just like Gramma Del, Ivory remembered and smiled. Her stomach churned with guilt as she remembered her anger at the prospect of no special gift this year. She realized now that her anger had been more inspired by the thought that Gramma Del might think her birthdays weren't as special now that she was growing up. The thought that Gramma Del had lost interest in surprising Ivory was what had really hurt. Thinking that she just didn't care as much anymore.

Well, Gramma Del was still the same, and she wasn't about to change. Ivory had a treasure map to prove it! Somewhere under this big red X lay something that Ivory knew better than to guess at. Gramma Del only gave gifts that were impossible to anticipate, and they were always just what she wanted. Except, of course, for those lacy bras.

She stared at the map again. That X, as unlabeled as it was, was clearly at the corner of First Avenue and Warwick Street, the main street running into town. She pictured the corner in her mind. The only thing she could remember on that corner was a brown gingerbread-house-type shop that sold crafts. First thing in the morning, she would walk down there with Rayne.

Ivory slept fitfully and reluctantly abandoned her dreams in the morning. But once her eyes were fully opened, and she spied the map on her nightstand, her mission filled her with energy, and she bounded out of bed.

Once Uncle Paul had left for work, she and Rayne were left to do as they pleased. A quick breakfast, which Ivory barely tasted, was done only as a formality, and she dragged her little brother out the door.

"But where are we going?" Rayne questioned.

"On a treasure hunt," she told him, adding as much excitement to her voice as she could. He was too young to be left home alone, so he'd better want to embark on this treasure hunt with her. Ivory had not the patience nor the time to coax him.

"Pirate treasure?" Rayne asked, his voice bursting with

sudden excitement.

"Sort of," Ivory said, pulling the map out of her pocket and holding the brownish paper up in front of them.

"Wow!" Rayne exclaimed. "I know where the treasure is!"

"Where?" Ivory stopped dead in her tracks. Had Gramma Del let him in on the secret? Had he known about the present all this time and not said a word to her?

"Right here, stupid, where the X is," he pointed and gave her the superior grin of an eight-year-old.

"Yeah," she sighed. That was more like it.

When they reached the craft shop, Ivory stopped and examined the map again. No indication as to whether the present was inside the shop or hidden outside near it. With this week's rain, she hoped it was safely inside.

"Hello," Lorraine Wekes, the owner, said pleasantly from behind the high counter.

"Hi, I'm Ivory Samson," Ivory introduced herself. "Do you have a package for me?"

"Let me see," Lorraine scrunched up her nose and pulled out a list. "What was it you ordered?"

"Uh, nothing, exactly," Ivory stammered. She hadn't expected it would be this difficult. "I was thinking my grandmother might have left a package here for me."

"Well, who's your grandmother, dear?" Lorraine asked.

"Philadelphia Flowers," Ivory answered, certain that with Lorraine's mother being friends with Gramma Del, she should have at least recognized Ivory!

"We got this treasure map!" Rayne piped up.

"Treasure map?" Lorraine leaned on the counter and raised her reddish eyebrows above the rims of her red glasses.

"Yeah, show her, Ivory," Rayne urged proudly.

With great embarrassment, Ivory lifted the card onto the counter, thinking she was way too old for a treasure map anyway.

"Oh, you're Del's granddaughter," Lorraine said in a sudden tone of recognition.

"Yeah," Ivory agreed, thinking that was what she'd already said!

"Well, she didn't leave a package for you," Lorraine said but added when she saw Ivory's face fall, "but it seems to me she was in here a few days ago and left an envelope for you."

As soon as she got it, Ivory tore open the blue envelope to find another map inside. Inside that map was another clue. It read:

TO CLAIM YOUR BIGGEST PRESENT YET,
GO TO THE FORMER HOME OF YOUR PET!

She read it aloud and knew immediately, even before looking at the red X marked up on Victoria Street, that her bunny, Jethro, came from the Digby pet shop. She wasn't fond of walking all the way up the hill again, but her renewed curiosity gave her a burst of energy.

She pulled Rayne out the door of the craft shop and gave a quick wave to Lorraine.

"I wonder what it is?" Rayne said several times as he trailed behind Ivory. "What's the biggest thing at the pet shop?"

"A dog!" Ivory decided. "It must be a dog."

"It could be a really big fish tank with a fish in it," Rayne suggested, apparently anxious to contribute to the mystery.

Whatever it was, Ivory knew Gramma Del; it would definitely be worth the trek up the hill in the hot July morning sun.

Chapter Five

"Package? No package for anybody," the chubby, red haired teenager behind the counter at the pet shop said. "But I'll check with Yvonne, the owner." A few moments later he followed a tall skinny blonde woman out of the back room.

"How can I help you?" Yvonne asked with a tinge of a French accent.

"Is there anything here for Ivory Samson?" Ivory asked maturely. "I think my grandmother, Philadelphia Flowers, may have wanted me to pick up something here."

"Like what?" The woman asked, confused.

"A big present?" Ivory asked timidly, realizing how silly she must sound.

"You have something in mind?" Yvonne asked.

"No, I don't . . . I mean, I think she might have left something here for me, but I don't know what," Ivory stammered, hating her grandmother for putting her through this, then instantly hating herself for hating her grandmother who was sick in the hospital. But why couldn't Gramma Del just have handed her a present like any normal grandmother? The instant memory that Gramma Del was as far from an ordinary person as one could get sent a rush of panic through her. She didn't know what she'd do if Gramma Del died. At least as long as she was participating in this treasure hunt, Ivory thought, she was doing something *with* Gramma Del. Gramma Del had set it up and Ivory was participating, just as Gramma Del had intended. Gramma Del wouldn't just stop playing in the middle of this game. She wouldn't leave Ivory just like that. Ivory *knew* it.

"I'll check out back," Yvonne smiled uncertainly and turned away. "A big box, you say?"

"I don't know," Ivory reminded her. "It might just be a small envelope."

Ivory and Rayne looked around the store while waiting for the results of Yvonne's search. Several glass cages, one above the other, housed hamsters and rats in the corner. A longer cage on the floor held two Dutch bunnies. Several glass cages held reptiles, chinchillas, and snakes. Two large tanks displayed various breeds of fish. The interior aisles were full of pet accessories such as leashes, pet foods, litter, and animal treats and toys.

"Nothing," Yvonne returned and shouted to Ivory from behind her counter. "Sorry."

"Maybe her grandmother brought something in when Lucy was working," the chubby teen offered, apparently anxious to aid in the mystery.

"I'll call her," Yvonne said soothingly as Ivory felt hot tears spring to her eyes. She just had to find Gramma Del's present. She just had to. Here she'd thought Gramma Del had forgotten all about her. Ivory hated her own selfishness as she pictured her grandmother going through so much effort to create this treasure hunt for her.

"Here it is," Yvonne came over and triumphantly handed her an envelope. "Lucy says a lady dropped this green envelope off on Tuesday morning and said a young girl would be in for it on Tuesday afternoon or Wednesday morning."

"Thank you!" Ivory said gratefully, feeling as if she'd just recovered a lost wallet with a million dollars in it. She took the envelope and turned to leave, preferring to open the card outside. So, Gramma Del had planted the clues the morning of her birthday. Ivory was supposed to have found them all by the next day. What if there were more clues after this one, and they had been thrown out in the garbage by careless employees when she hadn't shown up to claim them? Time became crucial now. She would not let her grandmother down. The thought of Gramma Del dying before Ivory found her treasure chilled her. What if she never found the treasure at all? How would she ever know what her grandmother had tried to do for her? How would she ever thank her? But no, that couldn't happen, decided Ivory, mentally shaking herself. Gramma Del *had* to get better! Gramma Del had always bragged about never being sick a day in her life. Ivory had to remember that. A person couldn't go from being perfectly healthy one day to being perfectly dead the next, could they? Gramma Del had always promised her that she was going to live to be 120 years old, and Gramma Del had never, ever broken a promise to anybody.

This time, the X on the little map was way down on the other end of the downtown area near the marina. Or maybe it was the fishermen's wharf, Ivory couldn't be exactly sure because the X was so large and sort of covered both spots.

She anxiously unfolded the map to read the clue inside. She read it aloud to Rayne.

"DON'T LET THESE CLUES GET YOUR GOAT.
THE NEXT CLUE IS WRITTEN ON A BOAT!"

"I'm tired," Rayne complained. "I can't walk way down there. And I'm hungry. I want to go home and have lunch."

"Okay," Ivory conceded, but only because home was on their way. Once they stopped for a snack, she was sure Rayne would be ready to continue their quest. This had to be the last clue. Anything beyond this would be considered torture and not a present.

She turned the riddle over and over in her mind as she followed Rayne silently home to King Street. She was surprised to see her mom's car parked in their driveway when they turned the corner.

"Where have you been?" her mother demanded at the top of her lungs as soon as Ivory and Rayne walked in the door. "I've been calling all over town trying to find you. Nobody knew where you were! I thought you might have been kidnapped or something!"

That was her mom, paranoid.

"I'm sorry, we went for a walk," Ivory explained. "Besides, as long as I'm with Rayne, you don't have to worry, nobody would want to kidnap him!"

Rayne ignored her insult and headed for the kitchen. The look on her mother's face told her this was not the time to try and lighten things with her sense of humor.

"Where were you?" her mother repeated her demand.

"Gramma Del's card was a treasure map," Ivory pulled out the clues from her jeans pocket. "There's a big present at the end."

"Your grandmother is in the hospital dying, and you're out looking for a present?" her mother screamed hysterically. "How can you be so selfish?"

Ivory felt as though she'd been slapped in the face. Tears sprang to her eyes and spilled onto her cheeks as a sob choked off her defense. "Gramma Del won't die! Don't say that!"

"She's very sick," her mother spoke evenly. "They're sending her to Halifax hospital. I came home to pack. While you were out wandering around, you could've at least stopped by the hospital."

Guilt clouded Ivory's eyes and mind. She couldn't bear to hear one more word of this nonsense. Gramma Del couldn't die! She just couldn't!

"Can I go to Halifax with you?" Ivory asked, knowing

the answer before she even asked.

"No," her mother answered, a little more calmly, but with tears in her own eyes. "You look after Rayne. Uncle Paul will be staying with you guys. He'll be home every day around 5:30."

"But can't I at least go see Gramma Del before she goes to Halifax?" Ivory pleaded, any thoughts of a present shoved to the farthest corners of her mind.

"No, honey," her mother said, softening as she reached for Ivory and pulled her close to her. "Gramma Del is very sick. She's already gone in the ambulance. I'm driving up. I was supposed to leave an hour ago!"

Ivory did not miss the intention of her mother's last remark and felt doubly guilty for delaying her mother.

"Mom, I want to go," Ivory begged, wrapping her arms around her mother and feeling like a three year old being left at preschool again. She felt so helpless staying home.

"Are they just sending her for tests?" Ivory asked with a sudden last grasp for optimism. She knew that rural doctors always sent patients to the city hospital for important tests. Even she had to go up once to see a bone specialist when she'd hurt her knee playing soccer. "When will she be back?"

But her mother didn't answer her, and Ivory felt her mother sob into her hair as they clung to each other in the middle of the living room floor. She wanted to tell her mother not to worry, realizing how worried she would be if it were her own mother that were sick. But Ivory knew her words of comfort would only be hollow echoes of some TV show she'd seen, and would never be taken seriously. Especially since she realized the loudest sobs she was hearing were her own.

Chapter Six

It was nearly four o'clock in the afternoon before Ivory managed to convince both Rayne and herself that it was worth the effort to go down to the marina. Rayne was more intent on playing video games, while she felt like a vulture. How could she possibly enjoy any present while her grandmother was so ill and her mother so upset?

Still, this was her only link to Gramma Del right now. If her grandmother did die, this would be the very last thing she'd give her, and that alone made the gift the most special yet. It didn't even matter to Ivory anymore what the gift actually was, it was already the most important thing she had to do right now. Even if it were just a note at the end of her adventure saying that the present was the adventure itself, which, admittedly couldn't be put past Gramma Del, Ivory would cherish it for the rest of her life. All her other presents from Gramma Del were experiences that time and memory could dim, or toys (and bras) she would someday (hopefully) outgrow. Even the brown bags with the pink bulky boxes inside would someday be all used up and there would be nothing left of Gramma Del for her. But whatever this was, Gramma Del had promised it to be the biggest and best present ever. Knowing Gramma Del, that could be anything, but Ivory promised herself that whatever it was, she would keep it forever!

It took paying Rayne a dollar for the candy store across from Fishermen's Wharf to get him back in the mood for the treasure hunt. They both bought drinks when they reached the store. Even the late afternoon sun brought sweat to their foreheads.

Ivory was disappointed when she found only one sailboat tied up at the marina, the rest were all out in the Digby Basin passing each other merrily. She was even more disappointed when a mere glance at the Fishermen's Wharf next door showed all the moorings vacant. On a calm, sunny day, the boats were out fishing, probably quite anxiously too after being kept tied up for several days by the wind and rain. Ivory knew this from hearing Cassie's father talk. He was a scallop fisherman and often bragged about Digby's scallop fleet being the biggest in the world and one of the major draws for Digby's summer tourist population. He also told a lot of sea stories, and Ivory knew that Cassie sometimes didn't see her father for weeks at a time.

Ivory's heart sank at the thought. All the boats that had been kept in by the foul weather on Tuesday when Gramma Del had planted her clues, could be gone for a week or two if the winds stayed down.

Her spirits could not be lifted even by Rayne's cheery chatter all the way back up the hill to her house on King Street. She ate supper in silence, even though it was her favorite, Kentucky Fried Chicken. Maybe living with Uncle Paul, who dined solely on fast food, might not be too bad after all.

"What's eatin' you?" Uncle Paul asked on Sunday afternoon when Ivory's moping couldn't be missed. "You look like you lost your best friend."

His friendly tone brought the confession out of Ivory. She sat at the kitchen table and watched him work on his maps, carefully measuring and studying photographs, while she explained about the treasure hunt.

"So," she concluded. "It could be weeks before the right boat comes in."

"Waiting for your ship to come in," Uncle Paul laughed, "now there's a classic case."

Ivory didn't see how he could laugh at this situation at all.

"It's not funny," she protested with a frown. "My Gramma Del may be dying."

"I'm sorry, kid," Uncle Paul said, still smiling. "I'm not making fun of you or anything, but don't you think you're taking this treasure map thing a little too seriously? I mean, we're talking about a senile old lady on the verge of death. She might not have been thinking quite right, you know? Besides, you shouldn't get your hopes up anyway, what if she took sick before she finished what she was trying to do?"

Ivory felt the blood rush from her face, and for a moment, thought she might faint right there. She hadn't even thought of that! What if Gramma Del hadn't had a chance to finish this, and she was just running around for nothing? What if Gramma Del had just started this and then forgotten about it? What if she should be in Halifax right now with her parents and Gramma Del and here she was running around like a little kid looking for buried treasure?

She opened her mouth to blast Uncle Paul with some sort of defense of Gramma Del, or some sort of reprimand for being so cold and callous, but nothing came out but a tiny squeak. She cleared her throat and choked back a sob.

"I hate you!" She screamed and turned to run from the kitchen. "You are so rude! How dare you?"

Ivory ran up to her bedroom and flung herself across her bed. She didn't even try to hold back the tears. Why had her mother chosen Uncle Paul, of all people, to stay with her and Rayne? She was quite capable of looking after Rayne all by herself.

She cried into her pillow until it was soaked. "Please,

God," she prayed. "Please, please don't let Gramma Del die!"

She repeated the prayer over and over. She just wanted her life to get back to normal again. She hadn't smiled once since her birthday on Tuesday, and if things didn't get back to normal soon, she didn't know what she would do. If Gramma Del died, things would *never* get back to normal. Her mother would go off the deep end and probably end up in the Nova Scotia hospital for crazy people! Her father would have to be gone all the time working, and she and Rayne would probably be stuck with Uncle Paul forever!

Chapter Seven

Monday it rained and hampered Ivory's efforts to search for her treasure. She'd planned on checking the wharf to see which boats were in. If she was lucky, maybe the boat which had inspired her grandmother's clue would be there. If not, there would at least be a few sailboats tied up.

Her mom had called twice over the weekend to say Gramma Del was still the same, which didn't mean much to Ivory because she didn't know for sure how Gramma Del had been to begin with. Dad hadn't called at all. Her mom had been sleeping at her dad's apartment that he was sharing with four other actors, and she said he'd said hi. Big deal! What good was a "hi" coming through someone else? "Hi," means you're pleased to see someone and talk with them. It's the beginning of a conversation. What was the good of sending someone a "hi"? It just didn't make sense to Ivory.

She watched baby shows with Rayne all afternoon and tried to ignore the weather and her life. She hated to admit it, being thirteen and all, but she missed her mother. She missed having an adult around. She wasn't used to being left alone for such a long period of time with only her brother to entertain her. She was even beginning to look forward to boring Uncle Paul getting home. This was getting bad!

Rayne asked her a question, but she wasn't listening. Her mind found it impossible to pay attention to anything, so intent was she on trying to figure out her situation. She felt as if the forces of gravity had suddenly disappeared, and she was left floating in the middle of space, and there was absolutely nothing to grab onto. Maybe this was why the treasure hunt was so important to her, she decided. It was the only thing that she could grab a hold of and hang on to while the rest of her world fell apart.

"Yes," she answered Rayne, not really caring what his question was. It was probably something stupid about the cartoon they were watching.

"You mean it?" Rayne asked in an excited tone. She still didn't care. She didn't even really care if his question had been could he go outside in the rain and dance around naked until Uncle Paul got home.

"Really?" He prodded her, now standing right in front of her, between her and the TV set.

"Yes!" Ivory snapped, but only so he would move. She wasn't really paying attention to the cartoon, but pretending she did gave her the freedom to let her mind wander. *There must be something I can do,* she thought, *something to make this whole situation better.* But what could she do? What she wanted to do was to get on a bus and head for Halifax so she could be with her parents. Why couldn't she and Rayne stay with Dad and go to the movie set with him in the daytime? Tonight when her mother called, she was going to demand it. At a time like this, her whole family needed to be together, not all apart!

"Wow!" Rayne exclaimed. "And I just thought that up all by myself!"

"What?" Ivory asked, focusing on her brother for the first time. Now that she'd settled her dilemma, she was ready to answer his question. She didn't want to hurt his feelings by letting him know she'd answered him without even listening to him. "Ask me that question again. I didn't exactly hear the last end of it."

"I said," Rayne said impatiently, rolling his green eyes in exasperation. "Is it true that your shadow is what holds you up and keeps you from falling through the floor?"

"What?" Ivory asked, failing to believe this could be a serious question from an eight-year-old. "Are you crazy?"

For a moment he looked stunned, then he burst out laughing. Ivory couldn't help but catch his contagious laugh and they sat and giggled uncontrollably on the couch. It felt good to laugh, and Ivory was grateful for her brother's comedic relief.

The question still brought a smile to her face late that night as she lay in bed unable to sleep. She'd worried all evening because her mother hadn't called, but when she finally had called, it was late and she'd only spoken to Uncle Paul briefly. He'd assured her mother the kids were fine, and Ivory wasn't told until after he'd hung up that it had been her mother.

Ivory fell asleep promptly after making a decision to travel down to the wharf in the morning, rain or shine. But when morning came with pelting rain and wind, she wasn't as thrilled about going out in it. Rayne, on the other hand, was enticed by such weather.

Only about four of the 120 boats were in, and Ivory and Rayne walked among gruff fishermen as they came off the boats. The men, old and young, in rubber boots and well-worn sweaters ignored the two as they went about their business. Within five minutes, the names of all four boats had been carefully committed to memory. The Grampy Joe, The Josie And Swell, The Pink Lady, and The Rob and Son Cruise O'.

How was there a clue in any of those names? Ivory had hoped for something that had the name of a specific place where she could pick up her next clue. Even a person's name that might possibly be a friend of Gramma Del's.

"What'cha lookin' fer?" An older man asked, spitting the words out of his unshaven face, dispensing a salty odor.

"Just looking at the boats," Ivory said.

"Well, with this wind, they'll all be in shortly."

"I'm soaked," Rayne complained.

"Come on," she told him, taking his hand and heading for home with the wind and rain in their faces.

Ivory waited anxiously until she'd finished the supper dishes before suggesting to Uncle Paul that she go for a walk.

"You're not going anywhere in this weather," he ordered, spreading papers out on the kitchen table again. "It's pouring out there!"

"But I have to go to the library," she insisted, knowing that if she told him the truth, he definitely wouldn't let her go. It was clear he thought Gramma Del was just a senile old lady. But Ivory believed in her. She knew Gramma Del had something special for her. She just *knew*.

"Well, it won't hurt you to wait until tomorrow," Uncle Paul said distractedly, studying his papers. "It gives sun for tomorrow."

"But, Mom lets me go," Ivory said, aware even this lie was a very weak tool. It was pouring out and windy, and the weatherman had said there was a chance of thunder for the Maritimes. But if it were going to be sunny tomorrow, the boats would be gone out again before she even woke up! This might be her only chance.

"Well, I'm not your mother," Uncle Paul said rudely. "There's no reason why you can't wait until tomorrow to go to the library! I've never in my life heard of a library emergency! Look outside! It's almost dark!"

It was true. The storm had made it so dark, the street lamp across the street flickered on and off, even though it was only seven o'clock in the middle of July.

"I'm going anyway!" Ivory said, testing her strength and stubbornness against Uncle Paul's authority. She'd had no experience with Uncle Paul and had no way of knowing if he was pushable or not. In this case, it was worth a try. If there were more clues to be found, she had to find them before they were accidentally lost by their caretakers.

"Don't forget who's in charge here, Ivory," Uncle Paul looked up. "I think you better go up to your room for the evening."

So he was testing her back.

"I mean it," he insisted, his tone growing harder as she stood there defying him.

She turned and stomped up the stairs. He may be the boss, she fumed, but he isn't going to stop Ivory Samson and Philadelphia Flowers!

Chapter Eight

Ivory flung herself on her bed and instinctively buried her face in her pillow. But she was not going to cry this time. Uncle Paul was *not* going to make her cry.

He was also not going to stop her from going down to the wharf. She knew that in the morning all the boats would be gone. She had to go in the wind and the rain if she wanted to see boats. And she had to go now, before it got too dark. She called Cassie.

"Cassie, you gotta help me," Ivory pleaded. "Can you come over?"

"Sure," Cassie answered with an air of maturity that sounded more like her sixteen year old sister, Sasha, than herself. "What's wrong?"

"We need to go down to the wharf," Ivory began, then realized she hadn't spoken to Cassie all weekend. "I'll tell you when you get here."

"Cassie's coming over," Ivory told Uncle Paul as casually as she could. She couldn't help add, "her parents allow her to walk in the rain. We are, after all, teenagers!"

"Yeah," he mumbled, not even looking up from his computer he'd just added to the kitchen table.

"Can I go meet her?"

He took off his square reading glasses and leaned back in his chair to face her. For a moment she expected a scolding.

"Look," he began, indicating he was ready to be fair. "I admit, I don't have a clue about raising kids. If Cassie's parents let her go out in a rainstorm, then perhaps I'm over-reacting."

"Can we go for a walk?" Ivory asked hopefully as her stomach coiled in knots. "We have to go to the library. It's really important."

"When she gets here, I'll drive you two over," he offered. "I'm sorry for being so over-protective."

Not wanting to push her luck, she agreed. She and Cassie could always walk down to the wharf from the library, even though it was way on the other end of town.

The unfortunate thing was, Rayne wanted to get out at the library with the girls, and it took an awful lot of convincing to get him back in Uncle Paul's jeep.

"Well, it won't hurt you to take him with you," Uncle Paul tried to reason with Ivory when Rayne started to whine and pout, the way he always did to get his way.

"Uncle Paul!" Ivory exclaimed in desperation, hoping it sounded like exasperation if there were a difference. "I look after him every day, all day long, and I need a break! I haven't seen Cassie in about a week! It's not fair!"

"She's right, Sport!" Uncle Paul said, pulling Rayne back in his seat in the front. "Close the door, we'll go watch a movie. Ivory, you call when you're ready to come home."

"Cassie's mom said she'd pick us up," Ivory lied and rushed into the library behind Cassie, with a huge sigh of relief.

"What's going on?" Cassie asked in an excited whisper after the girls watched the jeep drive away.

"My Gramma Del gave me a treasure map," Ivory explained and pulled out all the cards from her jacket pocket and handed them to Cassie.

"Cool!" Cassie squealed after she'd read them all. "So, the clue is on the boat!"

"But," Ivory warned, "I don't even know if there still is a treasure. Gramma Del set this up a week ago, and I didn't even open the first card until Friday."

"I wonder what it is," Cassie said seriously, biting her lip.

"Who knows?" Ivory said and bravely stepped out into the rain.

Together, battling the furious wind that splattered their faces with water so hard it stung, they made their way down the hill towards Water Street. Talking became impossible when Ivory's throat grew hoarse from shouting in excitement above the wind and traffic.

By the time they reached the wharf, Ivory felt as though her legs were made of stone. The dull evening light made it difficult to read the names on the bobbing boats.

"The Lady Clementine," Cassie read hopefully, shouting above the wind. "That's a song!"

"Yeah, but it doesn't tell us where the next clue is," Ivory reminded her friend of the purpose. She read the names of the boats she'd seen earlier along with the Sheila Problee Float, The Dora B. Getty, The Willa Lorraine, The Lady Elizabeth Higgins, Misty Angel and Annalee Swan.

"Here's The Katy Did," shouted Cassie. A flash of lightning and an instant roll of thunder broke off her next words. Both girls screamed and clutched at each other's arms, frozen in fear.

"I want to go home!" Cassie declared as the second flash of lightning crossed the sky with a sharp crackle.

"Me too!" Ivory screamed back.

They ran until they were tired and then they walked until Ivory was sure she would drop. Ivory panted as she pulled her leaden legs up the hill.

"See ya," Cassie shouted as they reached her driveway, and ran up her walk without even looking back at Ivory, leaving her to walk the last block by herself in the stormy darkness.

A crack of thunder spurred her uncooperative legs on. It was getting darker and she hated walking alone at night. She ran even though her legs were now numb. Her long, dark hair hung in soaked spaghetti strings down from her head and clung to her wet face. Her jean jacket was soaked through and she could feel her tee shirt wet inside. When she saw the lights of home, she could not will her aching body to run another step. She could barely walk when her shaky hand turned the doorknob.

"Where have you been?" Uncle Paul demanded angrily when she walked into the house.

"I walked," she panted. "Cassie's mom couldn't come."

"Where were you?" he repeated.

"At the library," she panted out in fear, almost knowing he could tell she was lying.

"The library called while you were gone," he informed her in an even tone. "They called to tell you they've had a book in for you for a week, and if you don't come and get it, they'll send it back tomorrow."

"Book?" Ivory asked in surprise. "I didn't order any book."

"She said she's been holding Robinson Crusoe for a week for you."

"Not for me," Ivory stated matter-of-factly and started up the stairs. She was on the third step when it hit her. One of the names on the boats today had been the Rob And Son Cruise O'!

Chapter Nine

Ivory stripped off her clothes; she was soaked to the skin.

The clue! She'd seen the Rob And Son Cruise O' earlier that afternoon! If only the library had called sooner, or if she'd taken the hint that her next clue could be hidden in the book Robinson Crusoe, this whole wet evening could have been avoided. She'd gone out and gotten soaked, lied, and been scared half to death by lightning, and all for nothing.

She pondered the sequence of clues in her head while she ran a nice warm bath. Why had Gramma Del done this? Wouldn't it have just been easier for her to just *send* her the gift? Why was she making Ivory work so hard for it?

As she submerged her chilled body into a hot bubble bath, she continued questioning Gramma Del's motives. Obviously Gramma Del wasn't as senile as Uncle Paul thought; a lot of thought had gone into setting up these clues. Gramma Del was definitely all there.

And the book. Would her next clue be hidden between its pages or in the story itself? She'd never read the tale, and if she had to read the whole thing and unravel its text, that could take forever! She didn't want to spend her whole summer reading about some shipwrecked man!

When the bath had warmed her then turned cool, Ivory reluctantly crawled from the tub and into a large pink towel. As she dried herself off, her mind raced ahead to the morning. First thing, she would rush to the library.

But when morning came, Ivory found it impossible to pull herself out of bed. Her head hurt, her throat hurt, and she couldn't breathe. The last thing she needed now was a summer cold!

"I'm leaving!" She heard Uncle Paul yell from the front door at 8:30. She rolled over, reprimanded by aches from every bone of her body. She drifted off again and slept until Rayne woke her up at 9:30.

"Are we going on the treasure hunt today?" He asked, jumping on her bed and breathing peanut-butter-toast breath in her face.

"Get off of me!" She groaned in a deep, thick voice that didn't sound like her own. "I don't know."

"Get up and move around, and you'll feel better," she heard Gramma Del's voice in her head. This was immediately followed by the soothing voice of her mother saying, "If you want to feel better, you have to stay in bed and get lots of rest."

Her body wanted so badly to obey her mom's remembered advice, but her heart knew it must obey Gramma Del's this time. She pulled herself out of her bed, her head aching with every step she took.

"Rayne, will you go get me the bottle of acetaminophen from the top of the fridge?" He disappeared and she inched her way to the dresser to pick out her clothes. She didn't see how she'd make it all the way over to the library; that was a good twenty minute walk. She'd be surprised if she could make it to the bathroom!

Cassie! Maybe Cassie could go pick up the book for her.

She crawled back in bed and picked up the phone. She pressed redial; Cassie was the only person she ever called.

"I'm sorry, she just left," Cassie's mother said. "She went somewhere with Sasha. I'll tell her to call you when she gets home, dear."

Great! Hanging around with her snobby older sister had now taken priority over Ivory's mysterious treasure! She crawled out of bed. If she wanted this treasure, she was going to have to do all the work herself!

When she was dressed, she went downstairs to find Rayne sitting in front of the TV.

"I thought I asked you to bring me some acetaminophen!" She reminded her brother angrily.

"Huh?" Rayne looked up from the cartoon briefly. "Oh, I forgot."

She ignored him and stomped into the kitchen, getting it herself. She took two with a glass of orange juice. She did feel a little better now that she'd gotten up and was moving, she noticed, thinking of Gramma Del. If only Gramma Del had been right about her period starting any day. Here she was thirteen years old for a whole week and *still* nothing going on.

The walk to the library was fairly straight, and Ivory was thankful it was on top of the hill. No climbing hills for her today, she decided. Rayne rambled on about something as he walked in her morning shadow all the way over.

"Here you go," said Wilma, the pleasant red-haired librarian, handing over the book with a smile. By the twinkle in her eye, Ivory guessed she knew the importance of the book.

She and Rayne took the book to a table in the rear corner of the library, shrouded by tall bookshelves to acquire a degree of privacy. She had to admit, despite the fact that she was now a teenager, this treasure hunt was fun.

She opened the book carefully and peered beneath its hard front cover. Nothing. She flipped the pages, then turned the book upside down and shook vigorously, anxiously hoping for a card to fall to the table. Nothing fell from the book and Ivory put it back down on the table, pulling her hands from it and into her lap. It was just an ordinary book with no clues. Maybe she would be forced to read the entire book. Or maybe, it was all a coincidence. Maybe the real clue had been one of the names on the other boats! Maybe one of those ladies' names belonged to one of Gramma Del's friends! She'd have to go back to the wharf and write down all the names. This time she'd also talk to all the fishermen. Maybe she just hadn't been industrious enough.

Rayne picked up the book and opened it to the first page. Then he turned it upside down and opened the back cover. There in the little manila pocket where the check-out card was, was also a small blue envelope.

Chapter Ten

Ivory pulled out the little blue card and saw that the front wasn't really a map like it looked at first glance. It was actually a large heart drawn with red pen. Inside the heart, Gramma Del's twirly handwriting scrawled, "TO MY DEAREST GRAND-DAUGHTER, WHOM I LOVE WITH ALL MY HEART."

Ivory could hear her own heart pounding in her ears as she opened the small card, holding her breath. Inside, in the familiar black block letters lay another clue. She whispered it out loud to Rayne.

"I WISH YOU COULD SEE THE SPARKLE IN MY EYES . . . BECAUSE I KNOW YOU KNOW WHERE THE TREASURE LIES!"

She read it again and again. It made no sense. If she knew where the treasure was, she wouldn't have been running all over town and catching cold. She grabbed the book and the clue and rose from her chair so fast and violently that it fell over. She put it upright and stomped angrily away. Rayne followed.

"Where is it?" He asked, trusting her to know all the answers.

"I don't know!" she snapped back at him. This last

clue wasn't really a clue at all. It was more like a joke. A very bad joke. Maybe there wasn't really a treasure after all. Maybe Uncle Paul had been right; maybe Gramma Del really was going senile. Ivory felt a sinking feeling in her stomach, realizing she'd just foolishly spent five days building up an excitement over some fairytale of a treasure. How was she supposed to know where the treasure was? If she knew, she wouldn't have needed a treasure map! She was walking so fast, Rayne had to trot to keep up with her.

"She said you know!" Rayne prodded. "Think!"

"I can't!" she snapped back. She felt like such an idiot. It was probably the book itself, Robinson Crusoe. It was a classic and she hadn't read it. Gramma Del was very big on literature and insisted on purchasing the best books. Gramma Del loved to read and had once told Ivory that if everything on the earth were destroyed except for books, it could all be rebuilt and regained, but if books were destroyed, life would dwindle to nothing. So, to Gramma Del, the book itself could be considered a treasure.

"The treasure could be the book, itself," she said to her brother, failing to conceal the disappointment in her voice.

"That's stupid," Rayne said, trotting beside her. "She wouldn't give you a present you had to return. If she wanted to give you the book, she'd have bought you a brand new one."

"That's right!" Ivory agreed, grasping the logic. "Gramma Del would give me something I could keep!"

"Not unless the treasure hunt was the present, and reading the book was just a bonus," Rayne reasoned.

"No, it couldn't be," Ivory told him, meanwhile realizing it certainly *could* be so, but she was afraid that saying it out loud would make it so. "Besides, Gramma Del said I *know* where the treasure is. But I don't!"

They walked silently home, batting back and forth ideas that were easily dismissed. None of them made any sense.

"Maybe you should read the book," Rayne suggested.

"The clue might be in there. Maybe the card was in the back of the book so you'd find it after you read the book."

"But she said I know where it is," Ivory protested, anxious to dispel the need to read the book.

"But maybe she means you'll know where it is *after* you read the book!" Rayne's persistence and logic annoyed Ivory.

"I thought of that already," she said, refusing to allow Rayne to think he was more brilliant than she was. After all, this common sense was coming from a boy who recently asked her if his shadow kept him from falling through the floor.

When she got home, she hastily made a peanut butter and jam sandwich for Rayne, and crawled under Uncle Paul's blanket left on the couch. She'd taken two acetaminophen that morning, but now she just needed rest. She felt so miserable, both physically and emotionally. She couldn't help the disappointment at the lack of a final direction. She felt like Gramma Del had just pushed her off a cliff and expected her to fly without any wings. How was she supposed to know what to do? She dozed off unable to come up with a solution.

She slept until Rayne woke her, shaking her and shoving her cell phone in her face.

"Mom's on the phone," he was saying. It took a moment for Ivory to fully wake up and realize where she was.

"Oh, Ivory, you sound awful!" Her mother shouted into the phone. Ivory felt comforted that at least there was somebody to recognize that she wasn't feeling well. Immediately, her body acknowledged every ache and pain.

"I just got a cold," she answered, keeping her mouth open so she could breathe better.

"Well, stay in bed," her mother said. "Rayne can help you out."

"I'm on the couch now," Ivory said. "How's Gramma Del?"

"Well, they're sending her back to Digby hospital," her

mom informed her in an unidentifiable tone.

"When?" Ivory asked with interest. If they were sending her back from the city, that had to mean that she was getting better.

"Tomorrow," Mom said. "I'll come home tomorrow afternoon."

Ivory hung up with her spirits slightly lifted. She could tell Gramma Del how far she'd gotten in her treasure hunt. She could just imagine the laughter in Gramma Del's eyes as she kept her secret. She knew that Gramma Del would not give the surprise away, if there was one. She would make Ivory figure it out for herself.

Chapter Eleven

After searching for the previous clues to take to show Gramma Del, it finally hit her. They had all been stuffed into her jean jacket pocket the night she'd gone to the wharf in the rain. When she'd gotten home, after her warm bath, she'd thrown all her wet clothes into the washer, including her jean jacket!

She ran down the basement stairs now, hoping that by some miracle she was wrong. Hoping that without thinking or remembering it, she'd removed those precious papers from her pocket before she'd thrown it in. But she knew in her heart she hadn't, she'd have remembered discovering that the rain had already soaked those cards. That had once happened with a math test, she remembered.

She removed her clothing from the dryer with Uncle Paul's jeans and socks. She felt her stomach turn into one big lump as she felt the hard, dry lumps in her jacket pocket. She pulled out the flattened and matted pieces. They'd been folded and now permanently preserved that way. She turned them over in her hand. The folds were now sealed and the ink had run and faded into thin pale lines and fuzzy squares. She carried them upstairs to her room with an aching heart.

Now that all the clues had been destroyed, Ivory

realized that they, in themselves had been important to her. Each one was a part of her grandmother. Each one contained the love and humor that made up Gramma Del. Each one contained hope for a promise and an adventure. Each one had been made for her by someone who loved her deeply. Now they were all ruined. And all because she'd been disobedient and lied. If she'd listened to Uncle Paul and stayed home, she'd have received the librarian's call. She wouldn't even have had to get soaked to get the last clue. The other clues wouldn't have been destroyed and she'd have them now to examine, to see if there were some hint along the way that she might have overlooked.

She sat down at the desk in her bedroom and picked up her chewed pen and pulled out a fresh sheet of paper from her drawer. What had been the first clue? She couldn't remember. She remembered it had led her to the craft shop. She racked her brains but to no avail. She tried in desperation to unfold the faded stiff pieces of paper, and finally managed to pull a couple of them open, leaving holes along the creases where they had been folded. The ink was faded, but she could make out the word *big*. Okay, she remembered. The first two clues had only promised her the biggest present yet.

She wrote that down on the paper in case she forgot again. The third clue; what was it? The need to remember it pushed the memory even further away. She closed her eyes and remembered opening the cards. Gramma Del's voice seemed to read them aloud to her in her head. "To get your biggest present yet, go to the former home of your pet. Don't let these clues get your goat; the next one is written on the side of a boat." Or something like that. That clue had been the Rob And Son Cruise O'. That had led to the book which had led to . . . well, nothing.

She carefully opened the last clue and reread it again.

I WISH YOU COULD SEE THE SPARKLE IN MY

EYES . . . BECAUSE I KNOW YOU KNOW WHERE THE TREASURE LIES.

Somehow the hint had to be in this riddle. She went over it word by word. She wished she could see her. That's it! Gramma Del wished she could see her. Maybe the clue had been placed in the book after Gramma Del had taken ill. She wanted Ivory to visit her! That was it! Gramma Del would tell her where her present was!

A tap at her bedroom door made her look up as her mother entered the room.

"Oh, Mom!" Ivory jumped up and ran to her mother. She felt like she hadn't seen her mom in years and couldn't keep the tears from coming to her eyes. She was so glad to see her mother. Ivory immediately noticed how thin and pale her mother now looked, and the dark purple circles under each eye.

"Mom, you need to get some rest," Ivory said, her chest ached like there was a great big sob inside of it.

"No, Mom needs me," her mother said in a weak, shaky voice as she clutched Ivory to her. Ivory had never heard her mother refer to Gramma Del as mom before; she had always called her Gramma Del when she talked to Ivory.

"Mom, I'm going over to see her, you rest," Ivory said, feeling more like the parent than the daughter. "Rayne's at the Hamiltons for the afternoon."

"I'll have to go with you," her mother said. "You don't know how bad she looks."

"But, Mom," Ivory said and pulled back to get a good look at her mother. She seemed so much smaller than usual, and frail. She was definitely thinner than when she'd left for Halifax last week.

Giving in to her mother, basically because she was boss, but also because Ivory felt miserable and sick, she rode over to the hospital with her mother in the car. Ivory felt her stomach coil in knots as they neared the hospital. She wasn't sure if it was a brief sense of relief she felt when a nurse grabbed her arm and prevented her from following her mother into a room.

"Do you have a cold?" The skinny nurse with black cropped hair interrogated her. How she could tell by just looking at her, Ivory wasn't sure, but she nodded, caught off guard.

"You can't go in with a cold," the nurse said. "It's hospital policy."

"It's okay," her mother said, putting a protective arm around her daughter. "It's all right!"

A second nurse, passing by and overhearing the conversation, stopped and grabbed the skinny nurse's elbow. "It doesn't matter for that patient!" She continued to whisper as she pulled her along down the sterile hallway.

Chapter Twelve

Ivory had known her grandmother was ill and old, but still, she was quite unprepared for the scene. Gramma Del was sleeping with her mouth wide open, and tubes going into her nose. Wires were coming out from the neck of her hospital gown and ran up to a heart monitor above her bed. An IV monitor stood beside the bed with two bags hanging at hooks on the top, holding what looked like water which ran down through a long plastic tube and into her grandmother's wasted right arm, which lay straight on the bed. A clothespin type of thing was on Gramma Del's first finger, emphasizing its boniness.

Ivory walked over to Gramma Del in the stillness of the room. The only sound was the slow rhythmic beep of the heart monitor. The head of the bed was raised slightly, so it was easy for Ivory to put her face close to Gramma Del's. She noticed that Gramma Del's hair was greasy and uncombed.

"We probably shouldn't wake her," Ivory whispered to her mother, turning to make sure she was still there in the quietness.

"We can't," her mother whispered as tears welled in her dark eyes. "She's in a coma."

Ivory knew what a coma was. She'd seen patients in

comas on TV. According to the doctors on TV, the people in comas could hear everything going on in the room, they just couldn't respond. She'd seen a movie about a cop who had been a coma for seven years and then just woke up one day and asked for a cigarette. It was a true story. Maybe Gramma Del would wake up any minute and ask for a bingo card.

"Did the doctor say how long she'd be in the coma?" Ivory whispered back.

Ivory's mother didn't answer, but choked back a sob. Tears were streaming down her face. She obviously thought Gramma Del was going to die, Ivory realized with terror.

"She's going to be all right!" Ivory insisted out loud, annoyed at her mother for being so pessimistic. Gramma Del was always all right. So she was in a coma, big deal. Ivory had seen many people on TV come out of comas with no problem at all. She didn't know what her mother was so worried about. Sometimes the voices of family members brought patients out of them. Well, now Ivory was here and as soon as Gramma Del heard that she'd found all the clues and needed her help, she'd open her eyes and tell Ivory just what was going on. After all, the clue did say she wished she could see her, well, here she was!

"Gramma Del," Ivory said softly near Gramma Del's ear. "Gramma Del, I'm here. I found all your clues."

She waited. Nothing. Did people sometimes sleep when they were in comas? If they did, how would anyone know whether they were awake or asleep? She reached out and took Gramma Del's left hand. It felt clammy and cold. Ivory moved to the foot of the bed and took the knitted blanket and pulled it up over Gramma Del, right up to her shoulders. Then she reached under the blanket and took Gramma Del's hand again.

"Is that better, Gramma Del?" Ivory asked. She waited for a squeeze from Gramma Del. Nothing. She felt her mother come over and put her arms around her from behind.

"Mom, maybe you should leave me alone with Gramma

Del," Ivory whispered. "I'd like to have a private conversation with her."

"She can't answer you," her mother informed her. "I'm not even sure she can hear you."

"I know," Ivory said. "I know she can't answer me, but she does hear me. I *know* it. Sometimes people come out of comas when they hear the voices of their loved ones."

Her mother smiled at her through her tears, perhaps thankful for the hope she'd lost while in the city.

"I'll go talk to the nurses," her mother whispered, and gave Ivory's shoulders a squeeze before leaving her alone.

"Gramma Del," Ivory said, a little louder than she had before. She tried to force her voice to sound normal, as if this visit was like any other. "I found all the clues. The Robinson Crusoe was the hardest clue to get. I don't understand the last clue, Gramma Del."

She waited, unused to having to carry both sides of the conversation.

"I love you, Gramma Del," she said, squeezing the cold, frail hand. "This is the best present ever."

She waited and hoped for Gramma Del's familiar squeeze, but the cold hand remained limp. She looked at the heart monitor. The white line retained its steady line with the small regular beep.

"Gramma Del," she continued to coax, determined not to stop until she felt her grandmother squeeze her hand, or the intervals between the beeps shortened. Even a flicker of Gramma Del's eyelids would suffice. It would prove she was still alive, anyway. She didn't seem very alive. Her chest was barely moving. Ivory jerked her hand away from her grandmother as the thought that she might be actually touching a corpse scared her. Then, witnessing the slight rising of her chest, Ivory took her grandmother's hand again.

"I need your help, Gramma Del," Ivory pleaded in a soft voice. She was determined to pull Gramma Del back from whatever force held her silent. "I need you! Your clues are too hard. I don't know where you put the treasure! I need your help! You've got to wake up, Gramma Del! Wake up and help me find your treasure! Come on!"

Gramma Del's right hand made a sudden jerk. She was responding!

"Gramma Del, I know you can hear me!" Ivory said in an excited rush of words as her knees turned to jelly.

"Time's up," a nurse with a smile said as she opened Gramma Del's door. Ivory's mother trailed behind her.

"She's waking up!" Ivory told them excitedly.

"What's happened?" The nurse asked in concern as she went over to the bed and pulled a blood pressure cuff off the wall. She put a stethoscope to her ears as she fastened the cuff on Gramma Del's thin arm.

"I was talking to her, and she moved her arm!" Ivory spoke fast. "She was responding to me!"

"Sometimes the muscles get cramped and the body just involuntarily jerks," the nurse said gently. "Her blood pressure is the same, and there's no change in her heart rate."

"But, as soon as I told her to wake up, her arm moved," Ivory insisted in confusion. How did this stupid nurse ever get on at this hospital?

"She doesn't realize she's doing it, dear," the nurse said soothingly. She didn't believe her!

"Watch," Ivory challenged and pushed past the nurse. "Gramma Del, wake up! Wake up and help me find your treasure!"

She waited in the still silence of the room. No one moved or even seemed to breathe, including Gramma Del. "Come on, Gramma Del! Wake up!"

"Ivory," her mother said gently. "Let's go. You're sick and you should be home in bed."

Reluctantly Ivory let go of Gramma Del's hand again. "But she heard me!" Ivory insisted to the nurse.

"Yes, she can hear you," the nurse pleasantly agreed. But the tone of her voice told Ivory that it didn't make any difference.

"Gramma Del needs her rest," her mother whispered in her ear and pulled Ivory away from the bed by the shoulders.

Ivory pulled back reluctantly, and turned away from the nurse. They shouldn't let stupid people work here, she decided silently. Everybody knew that people in comas would wake up if they were just given one good reason. It happened all the time. Apparently this nurse had never worked with a coma patient before.

Ivory followed her mother out the door.

"I'll see you tomorrow, Gramma Del," she called over her shoulder, the way she always had when she'd visited Gramma Del in her big white house on the edge of town.

Chapter Thirteen

The next day, as promised, Ivory went back. This time she went alone. Her mother stayed home with Rayne. The morning walk in the sun made her forget about the remnants of her cold; her stuffy nose and burning eyes were nowhere near as important as her mission now.

She used all her energy to display a healthy, alert smile to the nurse at the station on the second floor of the Digby hospital, so nobody would prevent her visit.

"Gramma Del," Ivory said in a hushed voice, drawing close to the unchanging form on the bed. "I brought you something."

She pulled the card that she'd made that morning out of the front pocket of her shorts.

"It's a clue for you!" she said cheerily, feeling like she was talking to herself. "Listen; your only granddaughter loves you with all her heart, and needs you to get out of bed and start; a treasure hunt prepared for you; because you're special and I love you too!"

Ivory admitted silently that she wasn't very good at poetry, but her great idea that morning just had to work. If Gramma Del had to find a treasure of her own, she was bound to get up and find it. Gramma Del wouldn't let a good opportunity like that pass her by. She didn't have a treasure for her yet, but today she would buy a present and hide it somewhere so that when Gramma Del got out of the hospital she could find it. Ivory would keep bringing her clues every day until she got well enough to go home. She just knew this would work. She felt it in her bones, as Gramma Del always used to say.

The body didn't move. Not a flicker or a flinch.

"Do you know where it is, Gramma Del?" She questioned, almost knowing there would be no answer, yet hoping anyway. "When you wake up, we'll look together."

She felt Gramma Del's hand again; still cold. She covered her up again. "Why don't they look after you properly?" she said in a stern voice, the same one that she'd used with her Jimmy doll years and years ago. Ivory sat in the arm chair near the bed, the one her mother had spent the day in yesterday and most of the night.

"Gramma Del, wake up," Ivory pleaded, clinging to the cold, limp hand. "Please, wake up. Everyone thinks you're going to die. I believe in you, Gramma Del. I know you won't die. I know how strong you are."

Suddenly the thought of her special bond with her grandmother brought an old memory back to mind. "Gramma Del," she began. She needed to know the truth. "Remember when I was little and I went to visit you? Remember when you took me to a magic field? You said it was a wishing field, remember? It sparkled, and I made a wish and it came true. Remember, I wished for a baby brother? Well, I need to know, Gramma Del, did that really happen? Did I dream that? Or did we just pretend it, and I later remembered it as being real? I need to know! Please, Gramma Del, wake up and answer me!"

She dropped Gramma Del's hand, feeling guilty anger well up inside of her. How dare her grandmother lay there, knowing all the answers and refusing to tell her? How could she leave Ivory never knowing the answers to so many things?

Who knew Gramma Del's secrets but Gramma Del?

She got up and walked over to the window, pacing in an attempt to dispel her anger.

"Gramma Del!" Ivory reeled around from the window in anger. "How can you do this to me?" She knew she shouldn't be shouting in the hospital, especially at her grandmother who she loved with all her heart, but she just couldn't seem to control her voice from escalating into a high pitched squeal.

"Gramma Del," Ivory continued, desperately trying to lower her voice. "I know there was magic at your house. I need you to wake up and tell me the truth about the wishing field. Was it really there? What happened to it? Wake up!"

She stomped across the room and leaned as close to Gramma Del's pale thin cheeks as she could. "Wake up!" Ivory ordered. "Wake up!"

"Gramma Del, please wake up," Ivory pleaded feebly, clasping Gramma Del's hand again. She sat back on the edge of the armchair and bowed her head against her grandmother's thin cool hand. She wished that by some miracle, the tears would warm the skin and bring life back into the dormant body.

Hours seemed to pass as Ivory silently prayed.

"Is everything okay in here?" The skinny nurse with the black hair from the day before asked, opening the door and poking her head into the room.

Ivory looked up and nodded, quickly wiping her tears with the back of her hand.

"Oh, honey," the nurse murmured, rushing to her. "It'll be okay. Your grandmother is just getting ready to go to Heaven, that's all. She's just having conversations with God right now, and getting things all sorted out between them so she can go live with Him."

"No, she isn't!" Ivory denied adamantly. "She's trying to figure out where I've hidden her treasure! And she's gonna wake up as soon as she figures it out! My grandmother isn't going to Heaven to live with God, she's going to come home and live with me!"

But Gramma Del continued to lay, unmoving and refusing to defend her position, while the heart monitor beeped its slow rhythm and the clothes pin on Gramma Del's finger glowed a bright red.

Chapter Fourteen

When Ivory left the hospital, she didn't go right home, even though she knew her mother was anxious to have her return to stay with Rayne.

She'd taken all the money out of her money jar in her closet, kept near all those brown paper bags, and stuffed it into her pocket. She would go to the mall, right behind the hospital and buy Gramma Del a present.

She roamed the aisles of the department store, searching for just the right thing for Gramma Del. None of the gifts she usually got her for Christmas or her birthday, like bubble bath or earrings, seemed quite right. It had to be something special that would make her wake up and look around.

Though every aisle held new things, nothing was right for Gramma Del. Nothing that would or could be called a treasure. She wandered into the drug store and eyed the fragile porcelain figures. A dainty figure of an older woman holding the hand of a little girl reminded Ivory of herself with her grandmother. That would be a perfect treasure. She paid for it and carried it out of the mall proudly in its small cardboard box. This afternoon, while her mother visited Gramma Del, Ivory would take Rayne and they would walk out to Gramma Del's house.

Realizing it was a much shorter walk from the mall which was near the stop lights heading out of town, Ivory decided she could make the trip quicker if she did it now and alone. She started walking briskly, despite the July heat and her nagging headache. She knew she could make it there and back in less than an hour if she hurried.

Gramma Del would be surprised when she came home from the hospital. Every day Ivory would take Gramma Del in a clue about her surprise, then when she came home, the surprise would be right on her nightstand. Oh, this was a great idea! Ivory's heart swelled with optimism as she walked quickly. She couldn't wait until tomorrow, and she somehow felt it could come quicker if she hurried.

When she reached the house, she walked around to the back of the house and retrieved the house key from the fake stone on the step. Once inside, the first place she headed for was the refrigerator. She quenched her thirst from the hot walk with the purple juice that Gramma Del always had mixed up for her. She left her glass in the sink as she heard Gramma Del instruct her in her mind the way she had thousands of times in real life. Then she went up the narrow stairs of the old house and into her grandmother's bedroom. The bed was unmade, which was unusual for Gramma Del. Her nightdress lay crumpled on the fuzzy pink mat beside it. For a moment, Ivory almost felt as though Gramma Del were just downstairs making sandwiches for lunch or something. The room still smelled of Gramma Del.

Ivory pulled the delicate figurine out of its box and placed it gently on Gramma Del's nightstand beside her pink glass lamp. It looked perfect. Gramma Del was sure to love it.

Ivory crept down the stairs, enjoying the stealth of the secret gift, even though there was no one around to catch her. She replaced Gramma Del's key in the phony rock outside her back door and began her trek home.

It was one o'clock when she reached her house and her

mother met her at the door with an impatient look on her face.

"Where have you been?" her mother demanded, with a hand on her hip. "I told you I wanted to go over to the hospital at noon."

"I know," Ivory said in an apologetic tone. "I just went over to the mall and bought a present for Gramma Del."

"Oh, that's nice," her mother said, softening noticeably. "Did you take it to her?"

"Not exactly," Ivory said. "I took it to her house to surprise her when she comes home."

Her mother's face took on an odd expression; one that Ivory had never seen before. Then she smiled a tight little smile and gave Ivory a hug. "That was very thoughtful of you, " she said. "I hope it works."

"Don't tell her what it is," Ivory warned as her mother grabbed her purse and car keys. "It's a porcelain ornament. I'm going to give her cards everyday with clues in them until she comes home."

"That's very thoughtful, dear," her mother said again, and again gave her that tight little smile. "I won't tell her. Rayne just left to go to the pool with Mrs. Murphy and her kids. They'll be back around four thirty."

"Okay," Ivory said.

"Can you make supper for you two?" her mother asked as she headed out the door. "I'll probably be gone until about nine o'clock."

"Yeah," Ivory said. "We'll have hot dogs."

"Great," her mother said. "I'll see you later."

A quick kiss and Ivory had the whole house to herself for the entire afternoon. She knew what she would do. She went to her mom's office off the kitchen and took the package of construction paper out of the school supplies drawer. She took it to the kitchen table with a pen. She folded a pink page into a card. Now, she just had to think of a clue.

She had it! She wrote in neat block letters:

THIS IS A VERY SPECIAL CLUE.
THE PRESENT LOOKS LIKE ME AND YOU.

Ivory smiled at the card and drew a heart on the front of it. She didn't think it was anywhere near as nice as the clues Gramma Del had left for her, but she knew Gramma Del would love it.

She went upstairs to her room and took out the only legible clue from her grandmother, along with the list of remembered clues she'd written down. Maybe if she found the treasure, Gramma Del would be so happy, she would just wake up and hug her and smile that warm smile she always had for everybody.

But the nagging thought that there was really nothing more to the treasure hunt than the hunt itself and all the love and care put into it by Gramma Del plagued her.

Late that night when Ivory heard her mother talking on the phone to her dad, Ivory hurried to her mother's room. "Can I talk to dad?" she asked her mom, interrupting the conversation.

"Yes, I was just about to come see if you were awake and wanted to talk to him," her mother said.

Ivory felt relieved to finally tell her father everything that was going on, the treasure hunt, Gramma Del's coma, and her plan to bring her out of it.

"Honey, don't get your hopes up," her dad said soothingly. "Gramma Del is very, very sick."

"I know that!" Ivory retorted. She wasn't some baby or extremely stupid person. She knew Gramma Del was sick. She'd seen Gramma Del, her dad hadn't. He didn't need to tell *her* what was going on.

"Well, she may die, honey," he warned her.

"Dad!" She shouted at him. How dare he think Gramma Del would just give up and die? Gramma Del would not give up. She would not die. She was just waiting for Ivory to find the treasure, that was all.

"Listen, honey," her dad said gently. "Just don't get your hopes up."

Ivory ignored most of the rest of her father's conversation out of anger. How could her father, one of the most intelligent people she knew, say something as stupid as that?

She handed her mother's phone back to her to say goodnight to her father, and Ivory to the solitude of her room. She stared at the ceiling in the dim light coming from the bathroom down the hall, until her mother came to her doorway. Then she pretended to be asleep.

Chapter Fifteen

The next day, Ivory went over to the hospital first thing in the morning. Even before her mother woke up. It was Saturday, over a week since her mom had taken Gramma Del to the hospital. She'd watched enough movies to know that some things in life happened at the most ironic times. She knew Gramma Del always lived up to ironic expectations. Just when everyone was expecting her to die, Gramma Del would wake up and say, "Oh dear, I can't afford to die today, I'd at least wait until after Monday night bingo!"

"I'm going to the hospital!" Ivory shouted outside her mother's bedroom door. Her mother grunted from somewhere within her deep sleep, and Ivory left.

She walked into Gramma Del's room just as a nurse was leaving with an empty IV bag. The new clear bags hung beside Gramma Del; her only constant companions.

"Good morning, Gramma Del!" Ivory said in her brightest voice. "It's eight thirty, time you were up and out of that bed."

She leaned over and kissed Gramma Del on the forehead. It was just as cold as the day before.

"Philadelphia Flowers!" She said in a scolding voice, trying hard to sound like Gramma Del herself. "Get up this minute! Do you hear me? I've brought you something."

Gramma Del lay unmoving, unchanging. Ivory grasped her hand, which felt even colder than the day before, and she shoved the card beneath the stiff fingers.

"Do you know what this is?" Ivory asked, as if she were talking to a perfectly alert person. "It's a clue . . . a clue about your present. Are you going to wake up and read it, or do you want me to read it to you?"

"Okay," she continued as if she'd been answered. "I'll read it. It says, 'This is a very special clue; the present looks like me and you.'"

She waited a moment, giving Gramma Del time to ponder the riddle in her head. Then she asked, "Well, can you guess what your surprise is, Gramma Del?"

Just then the door opened and Ivory's mother walked in, looking as pale as Gramma Del. Ivory noticed for the first time, how much her mother looked like her grandmother. She wondered if she looked like her too. She'd have to check in the mirror when she got home.

"What are you doing here?" she asked her mother. "Where's Rayne?"

"He's at Mrs. Murphy's for a few days." The answer was a monotone, and matched the drawn look on her mother's face.

"Why?" Ivory asked.

"They don't expect Gramma Del to be with us much longer, sweetheart," her mother said frankly. Her voice was small and barely audible. "I've called—"

But Ivory cut her off. "Don't you *dare* say such a thing! Gramma Del is perfectly fine! I've just been talking to her! Look, she's holding the card I made for her!"

Her mother tilted her head to one side, giving Ivory a look of pity. She reached out both arms to her, but Ivory turned away purposely, and moved closer to Gramma Del, clutching her thin arm.

She wiped a tear from her face with the back of her hand, and pretended she hadn't been interrupted. Why had her mother come? Why couldn't she just have stayed home? She didn't need to bring her pessimism here to thwart her progress.

"Gramma Del?" Ivory asked, as if she'd just missed something the old woman had said. "Did you guess yet? It looks like me and you. That's all the clues I'm giving you today."

Ivory leaned in as close to Gramma Del's face as she could and listened for any kind of a faint sound. Nothing.

"Do you give up, Gramma Del?" Ivory asked after a few seconds. "Okay, then. I'll have to bring it in and show you."

A sound!

A sort of gurgle sound came from Gramma Del's throat! She was trying to answer her! Ivory's mother was instantly around to the other side of the bed, and she leaned closer to Gramma Del's face.

"Mom!" she shouted. She grabbed the buzzer and pressed quickly for the nurse several times.

"Gramma Del!" Ivory shouted with hope. She was trying to speak! She was waking up! And it was all because of Ivory's efforts. She felt pride well up in her heart, for herself and for her grandmother. She knew Gramma Del wouldn't give up! She'd known it all along.

Three nurses rushed in and pushed both Ivory and her mother out of the way while they hastily pulled out blood pressure cuffs and stethoscopes.

"Did you call Dr. Watts?" one asked the other.

"Yes," the other said with a nod.

"Mom!" Ivory's mother cried in panic. Ivory didn't know why her mother should be so upset that Gramma Del was finally coming out of her coma. She should be happier than that, Ivory thought.

The nurses shifted their long faces from Ivory to her

mother.

"Do you want us to leave you alone with her?" One nurse asked her mother in a soft voice. So soft, Ivory could barely hear it from the other side of the bed.

Her mother nodded, pressing her lips tightly together, as if a great howl would come out if she didn't keep them perfectly sealed. Tears streamed down her face, and Ivory thought her mother looked as if she might faint.

"Mom," Ivory said in a confused tone. "Mom, what's wrong?" Even as she said it, Ivory felt it sounded like a stupid question.

"Maybe you should go home," her mother said to Ivory. "I'll talk with you later."

"I don't want to go home," Ivory argued as a sick feeling in the pit of her stomach began to grow, bringing tears back to her eyes. Why was her mother trying to get rid of her? And how come Gramma Del wasn't awake yet?

"Why don't you go and get your surprise and bring it in to Gramma Del?" her mother choked out. "She'd like that."

"Yeah," Ivory agreed. Her voice sounded like a hollow echo, and she didn't know why she agreed with her mother. Maybe because her mother looked so fragile, as if she, herself might die if someone said no to her. Maybe it was because Ivory's brain knew what her heart refused to believe. She couldn't bear to think the words into a real sentence. Just a feeling . . . a feeling that made her obey her mother without question.

She backed towards the door, confused and afraid. Then she turned and pushed the door open. "See ya in a little while, Gramma Del," she choked back over her shoulder.

But even as she walked down the corridor she heard the loud steady beep of Gramma Del's heart monitor. She knew it only made a little beep when the little white line jumped. If it were just this loud steady beep, she knew the line must be straight and flat.

She continued to run down the corridor towards the elevator. Tears clouded her vision so she had to punch the square button with the L on it several times before the elevator doors would close.

Chapter Sixteen

Ivory ran out of the elevator as soon as the doors opened. She ran past the blur of people and out into the hot July sun. She ran up the circular paved drive, out through the parking lot, and onto the paved sidewalk. Her heart pounded loudly in her ears as her feet pounded on the blurred pavement. She ran and ran; until her side ached and her breathing was reduced to mere inadequate gasps. Only then, did she slow to a walk.

But she didn't want to walk. She didn't want to give her mind or heart time to catch up with her. She didn't want it to sink in. She didn't want it to be real. Out here in the summer sun, it was impossible, just impossible for anything terrible to be happening. She must get to Gramma Del's house as soon as possible and rush back with her surprise gift. That would make Gramma Del better. That would make Gramma Del get right out of bed and dance around the hospital room. Ivory was sure of it.

She ran again. Memories raced with her of Gramma Del lifting her and dancing around the Christmas tree, and another, a long time ago when Gramma Del was in bed, sick with the flu for the only time that Ivory could ever remember. Ivory, only seven or eight years old at the time, had taken Gramma Del a present of tiny ornaments to hang on her tree, and Gramma Del had been so excited, she'd gotten right up out of bed and picked Ivory up and claimed that Ivory's love had instantly healed her.

Tears ran into her ears as she ran past pedestrians who stopped to give her strange looks. She barely saw them through her tears. The only important thing right now was to get Gramma Del's present and get it to her soon, or surely she would die.

She reached the house on the edge of town and with shaky fingers, retrieved the key from the fake stone. She remembered the time she'd accidentally thrown the fake stone at a vicious dog when she was about ten, not knowing Gramma Del kept her key in it. It had taken several hours of combing the ditch with Gramma Del to locate it. She remembered how Gramma Del had laughed as cars slowed down to try and figure out why an old lady and a young girl were examining rocks in the ditch.

"It wasn't bad enough my neighbors thought I was crazy before," Gramma Del laughed as she spied a neighbor peering nosily through his blinds. With that, she'd picked up her rock and crawled out of the ditch. Ivory had stuck her tongue out at the nosy neighbor and the blind slats had slammed shut.

Now she unlocked the door and stepped into the familiar home. "Gramma Del!" she called, knowing it would be her last time, and pretending it wasn't. She pretended it was last summer, when she was twelve. That was a safe time. The only thing she had to worry about back then was Maple Evans. "Gramma Del, I came to get your present."

She walked in and through the quiet kitchen. Her dirty glass from the day before was still in the sink, proof that the house was lived in. She passed through and inspected the living room. The newspaper lay open on the arm of Gramma Del's favorite green armchair. The crossword puzzle was half-finished. Ivory made a mental note to finish it for Gramma Del later. Right now, she had more important things to do.

She went up the stairs slowly, running her hand along the smooth, worn railing, almost feeling her grandmother's hand there beneath hers. Gramma Del's hand would never touch this railing again, Ivory thought abruptly, allowing her hand to caress the railing, trying to feel Gramma Del's touch.

When she reached the top of the stairs, she gave the top of the railing a gentle squeeze and went into Gramma Del's bedroom. The bed lay unmade as she'd left it the day before. Ivory pulled the covers up and fluffed the pillow. Gramma Del's bed should not be left unmade, she decided. She picked up the night gown that lay on the floor and folded it neatly and placed it underneath the pillow. For some reason, that was what Gramma Del always did.

Now that she'd helped Gramma Del make her bed, she'd better get back to the hospital as quick as she could with her present. Gramma Del was waiting for her, and it wouldn't do to keep the dear lady waiting.

She picked up the glass figurine and looked at it. Her grandmother would be so happy. This would go so well with all her other ornaments, yet this one would be special. This would remind Gramma Del, as it did Ivory, of the day she'd taken her to the magic wishing field. She chuckled in her mind at her childish belief in magic. She wasn't sure how Gramma Del had created it. Maybe she was a little magical after all. There was always something a little odd about Gramma Del.

Ivory walked over to the window and pulled aside the thick chintz drape. She knew she'd be able to see Gramma Del's favorite rose bushes and apple trees out back, as well as the two fields beyond the thin line of trees. She wondered what would happen now, to all this land, now that . . ..

No, she couldn't even let the thought enter her mind. She looked up beyond the rose bushes and the apple trees. Ivory's breath stopped in her throat as a glimmer in the distance caught her eye. She squinted in disbelief. Another sparkle flashed through the trees from the field beyond. She moved her head to one side, it must be the way the sun was reflecting on the old window panes, she guessed. But another, and still another sparkle peeped through the leaves of the old apple trees separating the field from the large back yard.

Ivory's heart jumped and she felt every nerve in her body tingle. She clutched Gramma Del's present to her chest and raced out of the room and down the stairs. The wishing field was magic! And it was real! She really had been there years ago! She knew it hadn't just been her wild imagination! She'd known it all along! It *was* magic, and Gramma Del had made it magic!

She raced out the back door and up through the back yard, her mind racing in a million different directions as her feet raced in only one. To the wishing field. *Oh please, God,* she prayed as she ran. "Please don't let Gramma Del be dead! Please let her stay with me forever!"

"I wish," she said aloud between pants as she ran towards the glittering field which was clearly in view now. "I wish Gramma Del will stay alive! For always! And . . . and I wish Dad would come home! I wish . . ."

But before she could even think of a third wish, she reached the edge of the glittering field. She was surrounded by sparkles as the sun danced around, landing on a sparkle here, a glitter there. As she walked towards a sparkle, it dimmed as another leapt out at her a few feet ahead. She looked down in front of her and there was a fragment of Christmas tinsel on the ground. She bent down and picked it up. Another piece lay tangled in the grass a few inches away. She picked that up. *How did Christmas tinsel get way out here in July?* she wondered in disappointment.

She glanced over the wide rocky field, with sparse patches of pale grass and watched the field glitter. Even though she understood the source of the glitter, it took nothing away from its beauty. She looked around. The magic was still there, she decided. It was *still* a wishing field.

"I wish," she repeated, trying hard to feel like she was five again. "That I could talk to Gramma Del. I wish she could talk to me. There's so many things about her I don't know. There's so many things I wanted to ask her. There's so many stories she had yet to tell me."

"I wish," she continued as she walked through the sparkles. "I wish that Daddy would come home and everything would get back to normal."

There, surely that would do it. The magic had worked for her before, it should work now. She smiled as she understood the magic of the past. Gramma Del had created this for her when she was five to find out what she really wanted for a birthday present. When she'd said a baby brother, her Jimmy doll was the best that Gramma Del could do. It had just been a coincidence that Rayne had been born. But who had created this for her now? Gramma Del couldn't have done this, she reasoned. Gramma Del was sick in the hospital. Deep in her heart, she admitted that Gramma Del was gone, but she refused to admit it in her mind yet.

As she turned slowly round and round in confusion and wonder, something caught her eye on the top of the hill at the center of the field. It was red. She walked towards it and when she reached the top of the small hill, her heart stopped and her head spun. She dropped down to the ground on her knees. About fifty stones, all painted bright red, formed a large X on a patch of dirt.

Chapter Seventeen

Of course! Gramma Del had prepared the wishing field for her as she had so many years ago. This was what Gramma Del had meant by her last clue. She repeated it over in her mind; "I wish you could see the *sparkle* in my eyes…I know you know where the treasure lies!" *Everything* sparkled here. She should have known! Gramma Del had thought she would know. Ivory felt silent tears slip from her eyes as the obviousness of the clue sunk in, and she mentally kicked herself.

She picked up an old cracked shovel that had been left beside the plot, obviously for her to dig up the treasure with. Tears soaked her face and mingled with sweat shortly as she dug, fighting away the images of her grandmother doing the same just more than a week ago. Her heart ached for Gramma Del. How could she ever live without her?

She stopped digging only long enough to throw the small red stones off the dirt patch and out into the sparkles. A few more minutes of digging and her shovel hit upon something hard. She dropped the shovel and squatted down, anxiously brushing away the loose dirt from the surface of a board. Scraping with the shovel revealed a wooden lobster crate cover. Ivory recognized it immediately. Its brightly painted seascape peeked through the dirt. Ivory tried desperately to swallow her tears. This was the thing that had been missing from Gramma Del's bedroom, not just Gramma Del herself.

She dug away the dirt surrounding the crate, and brushed off the rope handles. She tried to pull it up out of the ground but it was too heavy. What on earth had her grandmother put inside? And *why* did she have to bury it?

Curiosity defeated the need to pull the crate out of the ground, and Ivory undid the rope latch. She pulled a layer of bubbled plastic away to reveal a crate of books. Notebooks. Six stacks of hardcover notebooks had been jammed into the crate. From the looks of some of the ones on top, they were very old. Ivory burst into loud sobs as she pulled out the small pink envelope laying on top of the carefully stacked books. With shaky, dirty fingers, she pulled out a little card. It read:

I KNEW YOU NEEDED NO HELP FROM ME,
YOU KNEW RIGHT WHERE YOUR GIFT WOULD BE.
THE MAGIC IS INSIDE THE HEART, IF ONE LOOKS.
I GIVE YOU MY LIFE IN 66 BOOKS.
FROM BEGINNING TO END, HOW I'VE CHANGED, HOW I'VE GROWN,
AND MY TRIUMPHS AND FAILURES ARE YOURS NOW TO OWN.
PERHAPS THEY CAN HELP YOU AS YOU CHANGE AND GROW
AND I'LL ALWAYS BE WITH YOU WHEREVER YOU GO!
LOVE YA ALWAYS, GRAMMA DEL

Ivory sobbed loudly as she pulled out one of the top books that had a very old fashioned flowery design. She opened it and on the first page, in handwriting very much similar to Ivory's, was written: THE PRIVATE JOURNAL OF PHILADELPHIA BILLINGSLY. KEEP OUT!

Beneath the words was printed a date; August 5, 1962.

Curiosity pushed Ivory to turn the page, feeling a warmth of permission to ignore the keep out sign. But the first sentence on the first page caused her to slam the book shut and promise herself she would read them all as soon as she got them home. It read:

Aug. 5, 1962,

I TURNED THIRTEEN TODAY AND I STILL HAVEN'T RECEIVED MY SECRET MONTHLY VISITOR YET. MAMA SAYS IT SHALL START ANY DAY, BUT I AM POSITIVE I AM NOT NORMAL.

Ivory laughed and cried at the same time as she shoved the book back into its protective box.

"I thought I'd find you here!"

She turned and saw her father panting up the hill towards her.

"Dad!" Ivory cried and stood up as he reached her. He scooped her up in his arms. Ivory couldn't say anything else; no words could tell him what was in her heart as well as the sobs that drowned out his soothing murmurs in her hair.

"It's okay, honey," her dad said in a shaky voice as he held her. "I'm sorry I haven't been able to be here for you guys. I'm so sorry!"

She sobbed into his shoulder. It didn't matter what he was saying. It didn't matter how long he'd been gone. The only thing that mattered now was that he was here. She didn't have to be strong anymore. She could feel bad about Gramma Del. Dad would be there to hold her while she cried, and her mother too, and even Rayne. Ivory felt the weight of the past week lift from her shoulders.

Ivory tried to control the tears but they wouldn't stop

and it didn't matter. She wanted to tell him about the wishing field and how it was real. It was really real. She'd wished for him to come home and now here he was. She'd wished for Gramma Del to be with her always and now she would be.

Her dad allowed her to cry, silently stroking her hair. After what seemed like a very, very long time, he pulled her away from him and wiped her cheeks with his palms.

"Let's go home," he whispered. She could see tears glistening on his bottom eyelashes. "Your mom is home in bed, the doctor had to give her a sedative. I told her I'd find you and bring you right home."

"We have to take this," she said, nodding at the crate.

"Yup," he said, bending down and picking up the fragile porcelain figurine of the woman with the child.

"Um, that's gonna stay here," Ivory decided with a gravelly voice. "That belongs here, in the wishing field."

Note from the Author

Dear Reader,

Thank you so much for reading this book. It is one of the first stories I've ever written and still one of my favorites. I do hope you enjoyed it.

Stay tuned for the sequel to The Wishing Field which is entitled The Writer's House and will be out by the fall of 2022.

Feel free to check out my website at www.aspenfaraway.com .

Keep reading!
Aspen Faraway

Other Books by Aspen Faraway
Diary of A Teenage Mom Series by Aspen Faraway:
Book 1: Diary of A Teenage Mom
Book 2: Would the Real Mr. Right Please Stand up!
Book 3: A Real Family
Book 4: The Wedding Belle
Book 5: Wedded Bliss
Book 6: A Star is Born
Book 7: Choices
Book 8: Changes Happen
Book 9: The Glass
Book 10: A Meant-To-Be Love
Book 11: Just One Thing

Please visit www.havenstreetpublishing.com for more books by this author and others.